RIPLEY'S

RBI

FACT OR FICTION?

BUREAU OF INVESTIGATION

PUBLISHING

ISBN : 978-1-893951-52-5

10 9 8 7 6 5 4 3 2 1

Design: Dynamo Limited
Text: Kay Wilkins
Interior Artwork: Ailin Chambers

For information regarding permission,
write to VP Intellectual Property, Ripley Entertainment Inc.,
Suite 188, 7576 Kingspointe Parkway, Orlando, Florida 32819

Email: publishing@ripleys.com
www.ripleysrbi.com

Manufactured in Dallas, PA, United States
in December/2009 by Offset Paperback Manufacturers

1st printing

A SCALY TALE

PUBLISHING

a Jim Pattison Company

INTRODUCING THE RBI

Hidden away on a small island off the East Coast of the United States is Ripley High —a unique school for children who possess extraordinary talents.

Located in the former home of Robert Ripley—creator of the world-famous Ripley's Believe It or Not!—the school takes students who all share a secret. Although they look like you or me, they have amazing skills: the ability to conduct electricity, superhuman strength, or control over the weather—these are just a few of the talents the Ripley High School students possess.

The very best of these talented kids have been invited to join a top secret agency—Ripley's Bureau of Investigation: the RBI. This elite group operates from a hi-tech underground base hidden deep beneath the school. From here, the talented teen agents are sent on dangerous missions around the world, investigating sightings of fantastical creatures and strange occurrences. Join them on their incredible adventures as they seek out the weird and the wonderful, and try to separate fact from fiction ...

▶▶ RIPLEY

The Department of Unbelievable Lies

A mysterious rival agency determined to stop the RBI and discredit Ripley's by sabotaging the Ripley's database

The spirit of Robert Ripley lives on in RIPLEY, a supercomputer that stores the database—all Ripley's bizarre collections, and information on all the artifacts and amazing discoveries made by the RBI. Featuring a fully interactive holographic Ripley as its interface, RIPLEY gives the agents info on their missions and sends them invaluable data on their R-phones.

▶▶ Mr. Cain

The agent's favorite teacher, Mr. Cain, runs the RBI—under the guise of a Museum Club—and coordinates all the agents' missions.

▶▶ Dr. Maxwell

The only other teacher at the school who knows about the RBI, Dr. Maxwell equips the agents for their missions with cutting-edge gadgets from his lab.

THE TEACHERS

MEET THE RBI TEAM

As well as having amazing talents, each of the seven members of the RBI has expert knowledge in their own individual fields of interest. All with different skills, the team supports each other at school and while out on missions, where the three most suitable agents are chosen for each case.

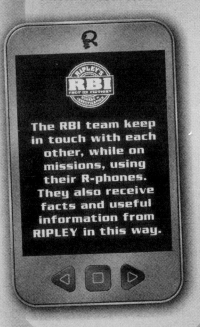

The RBI team keep in touch with each other, while on missions, using their R-phones. They also receive facts and useful information from RIPLEY in this way.

▶▶ KOBE

NAME : Kobe Shakur

AGE : 15

SKILLS : Excellent tracking and endurance skills. tribal knowledge and telepathic abilities

NOTES : Kobe's parents grew up in different African tribes. Kobe has amazing tracking capabilities and is an expert on native cultures across the world. He can also tell the entire history of a person or object just by touching it.

▶▶ ZIA

NAME : Zia Mendoza

AGE : 13

SKILLS : Possesses magnetic and electrical powers. Can predict the weather

NOTES : The only survivor of a tropical storm that destroyed her village when she was a baby. Zia doesn't yet fully understand her abilities but she can predict and sometimes control the weather. Her presence can also affect electrical equipment.

▶▶ MAX

NAME : Max Johnson

AGE : 14

SKILLS : Computer genius and inventor

NOTES : Max, from Las Vegas, loves computer games and anything electrical. He spends most of his spare time inventing robots. Max hates school but he loves spending time helping Dr. Maxwell come up with new gadgets.

▶▶ KATE

NAME : Kate Jones

AGE : 14

SKILLS : Computer-like memory, extremely clever, and ability to master languages in minutes

NOTES : Raised at Oxford University in England, by her history professor and part-time archaeologist uncle, Kate memorized every book in the University library after reading them only once!

▶▶ ALEK

NAME : Alek Filipov

AGE : 15

SKILL : Contortionist with amazing physical strength

NOTES : Alek is a member of the Russian under-16 Olympic gymnastics team and loves sports and competitions. He is much bigger than the other agents, and although he seems quiet and serious much of the time, he has a wicked sense of humor.

▶▶ LI

NAME : Li Yong

AGE : 15

SKILL : Musical genius with pitch-perfect hearing and the ability to mimic any sound

NOTES : Li grew up in a wealthy family in Beijing, China, and joined Ripley High later than the other RBI agents. She has a highly developed sense of hearing and can imitate any sound she hears.

▶▶ JACK

NAME : Jack Stevens

AGE : 14

SKILLS : Can 'talk' to animals and has expert survival skills

NOTES : Jack grew up on an animal park in the Australian outback. He has always shared a strong bond with animals and can communicate with any creature—and loves to eat weird food!

BION ISLAND

SCHOOL

THE COMPASS

HELIPAD

GLASS HOUSE

MENAGERIE

SPORTS
GROUND

GARDEN

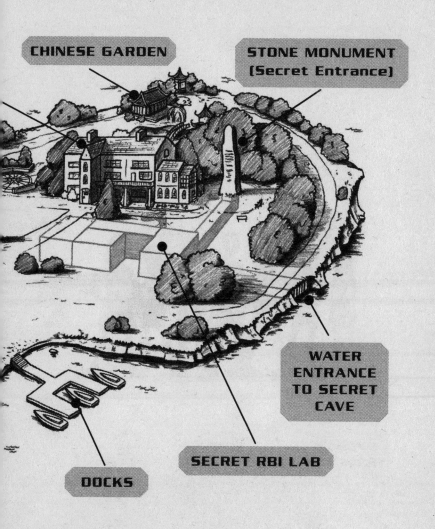

CHINESE GARDEN

STONE MONUMENT
[Secret Entrance]

WATER
ENTRANCE
TO SECRET
CAVE

SECRET RBI LAB

DOCKS

MON LEI

Prologue

"Bob, it's a monster!" the fisherman shouted, struggling with his fishing rod. "Get the net!"

Bob did as he was told and bent down ready to scoop up the giant catch. The evening shadows were playing eerily on the water. Suddenly, a scaly green hand emerged and grabbed the fish. It pulled with such strength that it snapped the line, dragging its prize back down into the murky depths of the swamp.

"There's something in there, Frank!" Bob gasped, horrified. "Something took the fish."

"What are you talking about?"

"It was a green hand—with scales," Bob explained.

Frank looked at his friend, his face a mixture of confusion and pity. Bob replayed the image in his mind; he knew what he had seen. The warm Florida evening had suddenly become chilly and he felt himself shivering a little. The sounds of the swamp now seemed unfriendly.

"What the—?" Frank began, but words escaped him as he began staring at the water. Bob followed his gaze. A deep ripple was spreading from their boat; only something huge could be causing it. The fishermen watched until the ripple reached the shore.

Their fish shot out of the water and landed on solid ground, followed by some sort of giant lizard. The reptile used its front limbs to hoist itself out, the way a person might get out of a swimming pool, and then shook its long back legs and tail dry.

The fading sunlight reflected off the creature's wet body. Bob felt fear grip him as it moved over to the fish, tucked up its hindquarters, and stood up on two legs!

The fishermen gaped as the reptile picked up the fish and glanced around, spotting them. Its eyes appeared yellow in the twilight and Bob thought that they seemed almost human. Letting out a hiss, it darted away into the trees.

Frank and Bob looked at each other in disbelief.

"I think we should go—now," suggested Bob.

Frank nodded silently and the pair quickly left, before the creature came back for seconds!

1

Ripley High

"Another boring class," complained Max, as he made his way to Artifact Studies. "I'd rather be on a mission than looking at old pots. I could be in the Pyrenees right now, skiing down a mountain on the trail of a yeti." As he spoke, Max ducked and dived as if he were really on skis. Zia giggled, and this was all the encouragement he needed.

"Or I could be speeding across the desert on

a quad bike looking for a two-headed camel."

"Ssh," Kate scolded him. "Someone will hear you." She had noticed that one of the boys in their class was listening.

"Nah, it's cool," Max shrugged, following her gaze. "He just thinks I'm talking about my holidays. He's got no idea about our RBI missions."

Kate winced. All the Ripley's Bureau of

Investigation agents knew that they had to avoid talking about their missions. Only RBI members knew that the agency existed. If all the students at Ripley High found out, it could cause chaos!

At 14, Kate was one of the youngest agents, but she seemed much older. Max, on the other hand, did not. He was also 14, but Kate felt he was immature and couldn't help breaking the rules. Typical Max she thought. She got up from her seat next to Max and walked across the classroom to sit, instead, with her best friend, Li.

"What's her problem?" asked Max.

Zia shook her head at him and the silver streak in her black hair caught the light. Max knew exactly what he'd done to annoy Kate; they often argued. He was smiling, thinking that he had won that round of their battle. What he hadn't noticed was that, as she left, Kate had called him a name. It was in one of the many languages that she spoke, so Zia hadn't understood, but she was willing to bet that it was rude!

"Yo, Alek," called Max, probably to tell him about all the things he'd rather be doing too. Zia sat down next to Kobe as their teacher, Mr. Willis, walked in to start the lesson.

"Silence, please. I'm going to be the only one talking now," he boomed, looking in Max's direction. "And Mr. Johnson, please remove those sunglasses. You're not going to need them indoors. Now, we're beginning at page 156 today."

The students opened their books. In Artifact Studies, they learned about all the amazing things in the school that Robert Ripley, its founder, had discovered on his global travels. Today, they were looking at his collections from the Orient, but the first 50 minutes dragged. The artifacts were interesting, but somehow Mr. Willis made everything sound boring.

"I don't think I've seen this one," Kobe commented to Zia, pointing to a picture of a strange skeleton with the caption 'Fiji Mermaid'. For years, the gnarled bones were advertised as the remains of a real mermaid. Even though Ripley proved the skeleton was a fake, created by fusing the skeletons

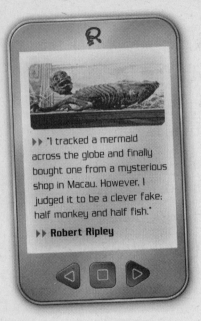

▶▶ "I tracked a mermaid across the globe and finally bought one from a mysterious shop in Macau. However, I judged it to be a clever fake: half monkey and half fish."

▶▶ **Robert Ripley**

of a monkey and a fish, he still thought it worth adding to his collection.

"I'm certain that this isn't in the school," Kobe insisted, his hand shooting up. Unlike Zia, he was a natural at Artifact Studies, and if he said that something wasn't in the school, then it wasn't.

"It might not be," Mr. Willis agreed. "Some

of the artifacts in the collection—"

"Sorry I'm late, Sir," a voice came from the back of the classroom. Everyone looked around.

"Stevens, so nice of you to join us for the last few minutes. What pathetic excuse have you got for me today?" Mr. Willis asked.

"I'm sorry, Sir. I was at the menagerie—one of the two-headed cows is ill," Jack began.

"This is not an animal hospital, Mr. Stevens. This is a high school," Mr. Willis told him. "And you'd do well to remember that; the last piece of work you handed in was a disaster."

Jack continued apologizing as he took a seat by Kobe and Zia.

"Perhaps you'll learn to take more interest in your studies after a detention tomorrow," Mr. Willis added.

Jack sighed and got out his books. Zia smiled sympathetically. She knew how much he loved animals.

"Now, where was I before I was so rudely interrupted?" Mr. Willis started again. "Ah yes, some of the artifacts are missing. They have only been seen by Robert Ripley himself."

"I wonder where they can be?" commented Jack, looking over Kobe's shoulder.

"Well, they're not likely to be in the menagerie, Mr. Stevens," scowled Mr. Willis. Jack and Kobe were about to argue when the bell rang.

"Yes!" cheered Max. Mr. Willis shot back an icy glare. The students gathered up their things and headed for the door.

"Don't forget, Mr. Stevens—my office tomorrow, please." Jack groaned as his teacher's voice followed him out the classroom. Suddenly, his pocket started buzzing, as did Kobe's—they had an R-phone message:

"Did you get the Museum Club message?" Kate asked. "We have to meet at the base." Mr. Cain always used the name 'the lab' when he meant the RBI base, in case the wrong person should see the message.

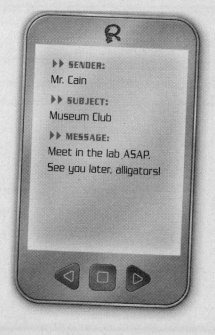

▶▶ SENDER:
Mr. Cain

▶▶ SUBJECT:
Museum Club

▶▶ MESSAGE:
Meet in the lab ASAP.
See you later, alligators!

"And he says to meet as soon as possible," Kate continued.

"Yeah thanks, I do know what ASAP means," Max snapped.

"Then maybe we should get a move on," Kobe suggested, sensing an argument brewing. The others nodded and followed him.

2

Strange Sightings

It was lunchtime, so the hallways were busy with students heading in various directions. The agents moved along the corridor that was lined with some of Ripley's weirdest finds. They stopped in front of Liu Min, the man with two pupils in each eye, from China.

"I wish they'd lower him," complained Li as she stood on tiptoe so that her eyes were in line with Liu's.

"You just need to grow a bit," teased Max, who himself was only just tall enough for his eyes to be in line with the head. Max paused so that his right eye was staring into the left double eye, which was, in fact, a secret eye-recognition scanner. On identifying the eye of an RBI agent the whole panel on which the

head was mounted would swing back like a door, as it did now.

Once the door was open, the agents rushed through to a spiral staircase, squeezing into single file to go down it. The school was an old building, but from the stairwell, everything was ultra modern. Motion-activated lights flashed on, giving the effect of daylight streaming in through windows where there were none. They picked out each of the agents, lighting their way down into the cavern that Robert Ripley had converted, first into a cellar and then into the base for the RBI. A huge, futuristic-looking black machine sat in the middle of the room: this was RIPLEY, the state-of-the-art computer system that stored the Ripley's database.

To one side of the computer sat Mr. Cain, who was deep in conversation with the most unusual feature of the RIPLEY system: hovering about 18 inches from the desk was the head of Robert Ripley. Not his real head, of course, but a holographic version of it.

"Hello agents," said RIPLEY. Each of the agents greeted him in their own way, and then they all turned to Mr. Cain.

"Thank you for coming so quickly," he told them. "RIPLEY has some new information on the recent lizard man sightings." Mr. Cain turned to RIPLEY, nodding to him to take over.

"The latest report is much more specific than previous information," RIPLEY began. The agents were always impressed at the way RIPLEY had been programmed to talk, not in the usual computer voice but in the way that the original 'Rip' had spoken. "These sightings were in Okeechobee County in Florida, so we now have a better idea of the area we should be looking at."

"Alright! Down in the 'glades," said Max, referring to the Florida Everglades. Max was from Nevada, but as the only American

student, he always felt a sense of national pride if their investigation was anywhere in his home country.

RIPLEY turned to a large screen and a grainy film appeared on it.

"This footage was recorded on the witness's cell phone," he explained. It was very jumpy, as if the cameraman was running. Shouts of 'Ohmigosh' and 'Man, it's huge' could be heard, but it was difficult to make out what was being filmed.

"His cell's rubbish," Max complained. The clip ended abruptly and the screen went black. "Did it eat him?" he asked.

"No, it did not," RIPLEY replied, smiling at Max's love of the gruesome. "The witness— 19-year-old Tom Perkins from Indiana, on a fishing trip with friends—later explained that the creature was a lizard that walked like a man. 'Believe it or not!' it matches some reports we have received, but no one seems very clear on what it is."

"Jack," Mr. Cain took over. "I'd like you to be part of the investigating team. If this turns out to be more lizard than man, we'll need your expertise."

"But what about Janus?" asked Jack,

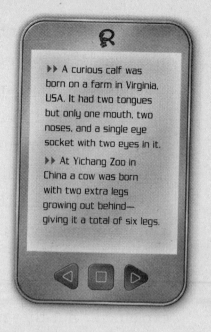

▶▶ A curious calf was born on a farm in Virginia, USA. It had two tongues but only one mouth, two noses, and a single eye socket with two eyes in it.

▶▶ At Yichang Zoo in China a cow was born with two extra legs growing out behind— giving it a total of six legs.

worrying about the sick two-headed cow.

"I'll take care of her," offered Zia.

"Well actually, I'd like you to go too, Zia," Mr. Cain told her. "The area gets electrical storms around this time of year, so your talents might come in handy. And Kobe? I'd like you to round out the team. For all we know, this could be a Seminole tribal practice."

"I don't think so," said Kobe. "The Seminole Indians do have a special relationship with nature, but I've never heard of them mutating into lizards. Of course I'll go, though—you never know what we might find!"

"Good," smiled Mr. Cain. "That's decided. Now, I want to remind you all about the Department of Unbelievable Lies."

"We know about DUL," Max sighed. "They're a bunch of spoilsports who just try to ruin our missions."

"I know you know about DUL," Mr. Cain explained. "But they're turning up more and more."

"Why can't they leave us alone?" asked Li.

"Because in the same way that it is our mission to find the truly unbelievable and prove it as fact, it is their mission to stop us," their teacher replied.

"But that's just dumb," offered Max.

"That it may be," said Mr. Cain. "But they do it all the same. I want you to remember— if one piece of false information gets into our system it would call into question the integrity of the whole RIPLEY's database and everything it stands for, including the RBI. Not only that, it could destabilize the whole network."

"Whoah!" said Jack, getting the point.

"That's why you need to be on your guard," Mr. Cain continued. "It's almost as if its agents know where we will be before we get there."

"Ooh, one more thing, Sir," Jack remembered. "I have a detention tomorrow."

"It's not Mr. Willis again, is it?" asked Mr. Cain. Jack nodded. "Fine, I'll get you out of it," he sighed. "All three of you have a 'field trip' coming up."

3

Gadgets and Gators

The three agents selected for the mission set about researching their location and the things they might need. While Zia went to see Miss Burrows, the geography teacher, Kobe and Jack went to see Dr. Maxwell, their electronics expert and the only other teacher who knew about the RBI.

"G'day, Sir," Jack greeted him, as he bounded through the door.

"Good day to you, Jack ... and hello Kobe," replied Dr. Maxwell. "What can I do for you both today?"

The agents told the professor about their mission, and explained that they would need to be tracking this creature in all weathers over difficult ground.

"Well, the first thing you're going to need is a thermal imager," he explained, pulling a device out from under the desk. It looked like a handheld computer console with a couple of extra buttons. Most of the things Dr. Maxwell found for the RBI were disguised as gadgets that teenagers would be likely to have. It made them easier to carry around without raising suspicion.

"The thermal imager works by picking up heat levels. See?" He pointed the machine toward the wall and a blob soon appeared on its black screen.

"Whoah!" exclaimed Jack and Kobe together.

The blob had a yellow center, with green and blue outer layers that moved with it along the wall.

"What is it?" asked Kobe.

Dr. Maxwell didn't reply, but kept the thermal imager on the colored mass as it reached the door. The door opened, and the blob glowed red, with orange and yellow around it. The boys looked up and saw that Zia had come in.

"The machine picked up Zia's heat," Dr.

Maxwell explained. "It couldn't sense her so well through the wall, but when she came in, all her body heat showed up."

"Ace!" said Jack, pleased at the technology.

"And you'll need night vision goggles, obviously," the Doctor continued.

"Obviously," said Jack, although it hadn't been obvious to him at all. He took what looked like a cross between binoculars and super-cool sunglasses and tried them on as

Dr. Maxwell turned the lights off.

"Wow!" Jack exclaimed, as everything in the dark room took on an eerie green glow. "Max has a game that looks like this."

Dr. Maxwell turned the lights back on. "Is it a sneak-'em-up game?" he smiled.

"Yeah. Have you played it, Sir?" Jack asked, impressed.

"Probably," came the reply. The professor was quite a fan of computer games. "Night vision goggles are used by the army, which is why the effect of wearing them is used in military combat games. In fact, I've got a new one that does it really well. I'll have to lend it to you sometime."

"Miss Burrows told me lots about the Everglades," Zia began, bored of the computer game talk. "She said the main things we need to beware of are the weather—"

"Well, we've got you for that, haven't we Z?" Jack cut in, still wearing the goggles. Zia smiled at how silly he looked.

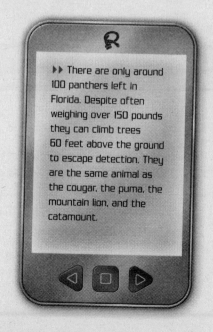

▶▶ There are only around 100 panthers left in Florida. Despite often weighing over 150 pounds they can climb trees 60 feet above the ground to escape detection. They are the same animal as the cougar, the puma, the mountain lion, and the catamount.

"And the wildlife," she continued. "Gators, snakes, bears, and panthers are all found there."

"We've got Jack for that!" said Kobe,

slapping his friend on the back.

"Not snakes," said Jack, shuddering. "I don't do snakes."

"Then let's hope we don't find any," said Kobe cheerfully.

4

Everglades Adventure

Less than 24 hours later, Kobe, Jack, and Zia were in Okeechobee County. They headed straight to the Everglades, the huge area of swamp that covers half of southern Florida.

"How are we going to travel through all that water?" asked Kobe. Having spent most of his early years in the African savannah, marshy locations still amazed him.

"An airboat," replied Jack with enthusiasm,

as they arrived at the rentals place. Kobe looked at the odd vehicles next to it. Each one had a raised padded bench on a wide boat base; behind that was a higher single seat with what looked like a long gear stick. The back of the boat was what made it so unusual though—an

outsized fan had been attached to it.

"Aren't they amazing?" asked Jack, clearly

impressed. "I've been looking forward to driving one of these beauties. They have them in the Northern Territory back in Australia. Dad used to take my brother and me up there and we'd rent one. They're loads of fun!"

Jack hopped on board and jumped into the driver's seat, as a man came out the office and walked over to Kobe.

"All set," he said, handing over the keys. "Your head office has sorted the paperwork." Kobe smiled: good old Mr. Cain. "Have you driven an airboat before?"

"No," replied Kobe, "but Jack has."

"That's good," said the man. "Just remember, they have no brakes or reverse."

Kobe's eyes grew wide—this didn't sound safe to him.

"It's fine," the man added, seeing Kobe's surprise. "The propeller makes the airboat skim across the water but it only pushes the air one way. Airboats are easy to use, though.

▶▶ Stripped down airboats can reach speeds of up to 135 miles per hour across smooth water.

▶▶ The top recorded speed for an airboat on land is 47.76 miles per hour. Some airboats use aircraft engines with lethal, spinning propellers with over 1000 horsepower.

They can go over grass, mud flats, and very shallow water. Where are you headed?"

"We've heard some reports of a strange creature around here," Kobe told him. "Have you seen anything yourself?"

"Can't say that I have," the man replied. "You could try Manatee campground, though. It's just a few miles in. If anyone's seen anything, it's likely to be the folk there."

Kobe thanked the man for his help before joining Zia and Jack on the airboat. He went to take a seat on the bench, just as Jack started up the huge engine and thrust the boat forward. Zia giggled as Kobe waved his arms, and then clung on to the seat to regain his balance.

"Hold on tight!" Jack shouted above the roar of the engine. "This is going to be one wild ride!"

He pulled the airboat sharply to the left as an alligator emerged to their right. Kobe gulped.

"Whoa, sorry big fella," Jack called out. "I almost didn't see you there."

"Are you sure he knows what he's doing?" Kobe asked Zia.

"Of course he does," Zia replied.

Kobe nodded, still a little nervous. The wind whipped past his face; they were certainly traveling at some speed. He had to admit that Jack did know what he was doing—the way he zipped in and out the mangroves, like a champion skier slaloming down a slope, was very skillful. It was all too fast for Kobe, and the boat skipping sideways made him feel quite ill, but he was impressed by the way his friend handled the craft nevertheless.

The airboat soon arrived at Manatee campground, where tents of different shapes and sizes surrounded an area of picnic tables. A campfire had been lit in the middle of it all, and people sat around it, cooking.

"Grub's up!" said Jack enthusiastically. "It look's like we've arrived at lunchtime."

The agents introduced themselves to the

group of campers, explaining that they were on the trail of the lizard man.

"I saw something strange," a camper named Bob told them. "I was fishing one evening with my friend, Frank, when our catch got grabbed by something scaly. It looked like a lizard, but it walked on two legs. It took the fish and ran away."

▶▶ Dave Romero, a fisherman from Pennsylvania, USA, has caught more than 25,000 bass! He keeps a journal detailing every bass he has ever hooked.

▶▶ In 2009, an 11-year-old British girl weighing 84 pounds caught a catfish weighing 193 pounds.

"I saw it too," said a second man, "but it was early morning. I could see a green hand grasping a branch and eyes peering out from the mangroves. I didn't move, in case it came after me, and then it just disappeared. One second it was there, the next it was gone."

The three agents interviewed all the campers,

with Jack typically doing a fair bit of eating too! Kobe found one man who seemed clear on what he had seen. He called the other two over to hear his story.

"I was fishing when I saw it," the man began, his eyes wide. Zia studied his big fishing hat, shiny black shoes and cargo shorts. He also wore a fishing vest, its many pockets stuffed with wriggling worms to use as bait. "The thing just crawled out of the lake—it was huge! But I would say it was much more like a panther than a lizard ... a water panther, perhaps?"

Jack shook his head; he had never heard of a water panther.

"It looked really mean," the man went on. "It had glowing red eyes and giant claws ... and its teeth! Wow, its teeth were terrifying when it snarled. They were sharp spikes, with bits of rotting food stuck between them. It started to charge, so I scrambled up a tree and waited for it to lose interest."

Jack frowned. If the creature were any sort of panther, it would have climbed up after the fisherman.

"Where was this?" Zia asked. Jack saw that she was skeptical too.

"Oh, way over there," the man replied, pointing into the distance. "Closer to Everglades County."

The agents were slightly confused. This report

went against everything the RBI had received. The area was different, this creature was like a panther, and no one had said that the creature attacked people.

"A water panther?" Jack repeated, as they headed back to the boat. "I don't think that sounds right."

"Neither do I," Zia agreed. "There was something about that man I didn't trust." She paused and thought for a moment. "No, I just can't put my thumb on it."

"Finger," Jack corrected her English. "The saying is 'I just can't put my finger on it'."

"Thank you," Zia blushed. "Your language is so strange." Jack nodded. He often found it hard to understand Kate and Max, and they were all supposed to speak the same language!

"I think we should stick to our original plan," said Kobe. "Then we can move to Everglades County if we have no luck." He took a deep breath and stepped on to the deck—he was not looking forward to another ride.

"Woo hoo!" yelled Jack, as he gunned the airboat and the agents soared away from the campground.

5

Airboat Chase

Not long after they set off, another airboat appeared. Following the rules of sensible airboat driving, Jack slowed down.

"Howdy, y'all," its two passengers called to them. Zia wasn't sure if it was the roar of the engines or the echo from the mangroves, but their accents sounded false, like when Kate tried to wind Max up by copying his accent.

"Have you guys come from Manatee

campground?" one asked. Their boat was laden with fishing tackle, and a bucket of bait was sitting on the deck. As they slowed down, fishy goo slopped over the edge of the bucket and on to the other man's polished black shoes.

"Eugh!" he exclaimed. "These are my best shoes! That's going to be a nightmare to clean off."

"Yes, we were just there," Jack shouted back. "We're just looking for somewhere to set up camp."

"There are some good places over there, near Everglades County," the first man suggested.

"And there's some great fishing holes too," added the man with the fishy shoes. "We could show you where to go, and even lend you some of our equipment. We were hoping to see the strange big cat that's been seen over there, but it didn't show. Maybe if we all went back together we might be luckier?"

"No thanks, we're fine going this way,"

Jack told them, gently speeding up.

"There's nothing worth seeing that way. You're going to miss out," the man shouted after them.

"That was weird," Jack said. "They didn't want us to go this way."

"I know," said Zia. "They were a bit strange. They reminded me of that man from the campsite."

"Yes," Kobe agreed, still clinging to his seat. "They wanted us to go to Everglades County, too. I wonder what's there?"

Kobe didn't get an answer, as another airboat rumbled toward them. The engines were loud enough by themselves, but the echo off the mangrove trees made them sound like thunder.

"Don't people know you're supposed to slow down when there's another airboat nearby?" Jack asked, shouting to be heard over the noise. They had entered an area of tall grasses, making it impossible to see where the other airboat was. Suddenly, it appeared from a side channel, and cut across their path so that Jack had to swerve quickly to avoid hitting it.

"It's those fishermen again," Kobe said. "They're chasing us!"

"Why would they be doing that?" Jack shouted.

"Their shoes are wrong!" Zia suddenly exclaimed. "How many fishermen do you know who wear shiny black shoes? The man at the campground wore them, too."

"Yeah, why would fishermen polish their shoes?" asked Jack, starting to pull away from the airboat that had just reappeared behind them.

"They wouldn't," Zia explained. "But DUL agents would! We need to get out of here. Speed up!"

Jack quickly pulled the airboat deeper into the swamplands, heading for a narrow canal and changing course in an instant to shoot around a tree. Zia saw Kobe turn a shade of green as Jack expertly followed the maze of channels, the airboat skimming the surface like a pond skater.

"They're gaining on us," Zia warned Jack. He reacted immediately; the airboat jumped over a mangrove root, and he swiftly changed

direction, hoping to throw the DUL agents off the trail.

But they kept following.

Jack zigged and zagged, changing channels and switching direction, but the DUL airboat was matching him and closing the gap between them.

"Hang on!" Jack called to the other two.

"This is going to be a tight one." He swung the boat right around and sped straight through a narrow gap between two trees. Hearing Zia cry out, he thought that the sharp corner was too much for her, but he soon realized she was screaming Kobe's name.

"Kobe's fallen in!" she yelled. "You have to go back."

Jack turned to see his friend's head bobbing in the swampy water, growing smaller and smaller as the airboat raced away. He could also see that Kobe was right in the DUL boat's path.

"I'll loop back around," he told Zia, "but I can't slow down much or that DUL airboat is going to hit Kobe. You're going to have to lean out and grab him, okay?"

Zia nodded, moving over to the side of the boat.

"Ready," she called out.

Jack slowed the airboat for a second as he changed direction—he didn't want Zia falling overboard too—and then sped up toward the tiny speck in the distance that was Kobe.

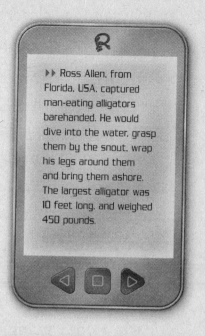

▶▶ Ross Allen, from Florida, USA, captured man-eating alligators barehanded. He would dive into the water, grasp them by the snout, wrap his legs around them and bring them ashore. The largest alligator was 10 feet long, and weighed 450 pounds.

Kobe had started to panic the moment he hit the water. Having only learned to swim when he started at Ripley High, he still wasn't very experienced. He tried to tread water, but he kept feeling something scratching at his foot. He remembered the gator that they had almost hit earlier, and the story that the fisherman had told him .... Pull yourself together, he thought, you're an RBI agent.

He saw Jack's airboat turn around, just as he felt something hard brush against his leg. The airboat sounded closer than it looked; then he realized it was the DUL airboat behind him! It was headed toward him from one direction, while Jack and Zia were coming at him from the other; this was going to be close!

Kobe readied himself to leap on to the boat as it passed; his timing was going to have to be perfect. He felt around with his foot: there was a submerged root that he could push himself off. He bent his knees and let his head go under the water, ready to thrust himself into the air ....

"Jack, Kobe's going under!" Zia cried. "He can't swim very well, he's drowning!"

"We're nearly there, Z," Jack reassured her.

Zia watched as Kobe's head disappeared and only bubbles remained on the surface. When the airboat reached the spot where he had been, she took a deep breath and leaned forward, expecting to haul out his limp body. Suddenly, the water erupted and Kobe flew at her amid a shower of spray so that they both

tumbled into the boat in a tangle of limbs. Zia looked at Kobe with shock and relief.

"Thank goodness," he gasped. "I thought there was a gator after me."

"There was a gator after you," Zia told him, her face white. "As you landed on the boat it jumped out after you and just missed your feet!"

Kobe swallowed hard—perhaps it wasn't a root he'd put his foot on after all!

"Okay, hang on. We're off again," said Jack, quickly weaving the airboat through the mangroves—the DUL airboat was now closer than ever!

6

Silence in the Swampland

The DUL airboat cut straight across their path, trying to block their exit. Jack slammed his foot down on the rudder pedal, spinning the boat around. As it turned, a huge wave of spray drenched the other craft and momentarily blinded the DUL agents, so that Jack could escape deeper into the Everglades. When they reached an area of dense reeds, he cut the engine and allowed the airboat to coast.

"Why are you stopping?" hissed Zia. "They'll catch us!"

"They won't see us here," Jack whispered, "and if they can't hear the engine, they'll think we've left."

Zia watched the other airboat come into view. The DUL agents listened and continued slowly on, peering through trees and mangroves, hoping to find their prey.

Almost half an hour passed before Jack was happy that they had lost the DUL agents. The light was starting to fade.

"We should stop soon," said Kobe "I don't think we should be riding through the Everglades in the dark, we might hit something."

"We'll make camp here," Jack told him, knowing that Kobe would rather not be driving through the Everglades at any time of day! He tied off the boat while the other two set up camp, and then all three cooked some of their provisions.

▶▶ A man in Turkey has become addicted to eating live scorpions. He has eaten them since childhood and villagers help him search for fresh supplies.

▶▶ 'The worm man' in Sydney, Australia eats live earthworms, either in sandwiches, or just plain.

"We didn't need to bring half this much," Jack pointed out. "The Everglades are full of nutritious plants and insect life—"

"You mean bugs, don't you?" Zia interrupted.

"Well, yeah," Jack agreed. "But they're yummy bugs!"

Zia pulled a face; bugs didn't sound like a tasty treat to her!

After they had finished eating, Jack told a spooky story.

"Years ago, there was a young Seminole girl named Hachi, meaning 'Stream', because of her love of water. One day, she was swimming in one of the Everglades lakes. Everything around her was silent except for the gentle sounds of the swamp creatures and the rustle of the light breeze in the trees. Stream swam here every day before helping her mother make dinner.

However, on this particular day, Stream did not go home. A search party was sent out and they found the girl just before sunset, lying face down in the pool; the spiny roots of the creeping lake-flower, a hyacinth-like plant, had tangled themselves around her limbs and pulled her under the water.

Stream's family took her death as sign that nature no longer wanted man living so closely, and they moved far away. Others suggested that the plant had evolved and selected Stream as its first victim. Now, it would never stop searching for prey.

Either way, the creeping lake-flower still blooms in the Everglades today. It is said that if you swim too close to it, the wind sounds like the cry of a young girl—of Stream warning victims so that they might escape her watery fate."

▶▶ The creeping lake-flower, a hyacinth-like plant, floats on the surface of the water. It is one of the fastest growing plants in the world, and grows so quickly that it often causes blockages in waterways. It can double its growth in only two weeks—and one acre of plants can weigh up to an amazing 200 tons!

"Wow, is that true?" asked Zia, a little concerned.

"Well, some of it is," Jack replied. "The rest I added for effect. But the creeping lake-flower really does trap anything with its spiny roots."

"Lovely," said Zia, eyeing the plants suspiciously as she crawled into her tent. Although she'd set it up as far away from Jack's as she could, with Kobe's tent in the middle, Zia heard Jack start snoring almost immediately. Kobe's even breathing, which seemed almost as loud, told her that he had fallen asleep soon after, but Zia couldn't relax. The sounds of the swampland crept in through the thin fabric of her tent. Every time she thought she might drift off to sleep, an animal's screech or cry made her jump.

When Zia heard twigs snapping, she got to her feet and picked up her flashlight. She edged toward the door, thinking that it was probably one of the boys looking for a midnight snack—Jack, most likely! But for some reason, she didn't dare turn on the flashlight. Instead, she picked up the heat-sensing device that Dr. Maxwell had given them; it registered a person's heat signature outside. Gotcha Jack, she thought, but then the moon came out and cast a silhouette on the wall of her tent. The figure turned sideways and Zia's eyes widened— at the base of its body was a tail. It was some sort of lizard! The scream Zia had been trying to stop crept out, shattering the silence. The

shadow froze for a second before disappearing and the boys appeared in its place. Zia screamed again: they were wearing night-vision goggles and looked quite bizarre. She relaxed as Jack pulled his goggles off his head.

"Did you see it?" she asked.

"See what?"

"The thing," Zia explained. "It looked like a lizard of some sort, but it glowed like a person on the heat sensor."

"Z, there's nothing out there," Jack assured her. "You must have been dreaming. Maybe that story scared you?"

"I wasn't dreaming," Zia argued.

"Well, there's definitely nothing there," said Kobe. "Get some sleep and I'm sure you'll feel better in the morning."

The next day, Zia awoke to the sound of raised voices. She stepped out into the morning sun to see Kobe and Jack searching the bags.

"Well, it must be here somewhere," said Jack.

"It isn't, I've looked," Kobe insisted.

"What isn't?" asked Zia.

"I went to make breakfast and all our food had gone," Kobe told her.

"I told you!" she exclaimed. "Whatever I saw last night must have taken our food."

The boys still thought that Zia's mind had been playing tricks on her, although they had to admit that something had taken their food. They all agreed that they needed to be on constant alert.

"We'll leave the airboat here today and go on foot," Jack told the others. "We're in the right sort of area now, and the airboat will just scare lots of the wildlife away."

"Good idea," said Zia. "There's a storm coming today, too. It will be best if we're out of the water."

Kobe smiled; he'd enjoy not feeling nauseous

all day. As they walked, he found that the Everglades seemed much friendlier when he was not whizzing by at breathtaking speeds. He had to admit it really was a beautiful place. They made their way over islands of mangrove roots and parts that reminded him of the savannah back in Kenya, with long sawgrass and areas of shorter grasses that moved in the breeze like a free-flowing river. All this was surrounded by

enormous amounts of water; water that you couldn't see or hear, but which Kobe knew flowed constantly, making the rich ecosystem that is the Everglades.

The variety of wildlife also fascinated him. Beautiful water lilies bloomed everywhere and brightly colored flowers peeped out between the lush green leaves. An amazing number of birds flew above them, and the air was thick with the calls of frogs and toads. Kobe thought that all the animal noises sounded so welcoming ....

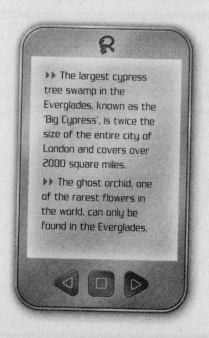

▶▶ The largest cypress tree swamp in the Everglades, known as the 'Big Cypress', is twice the size of the entire city of London and covers over 2000 square miles.

▶▶ The ghost orchid, one of the rarest flowers in the world, can only be found in the Everglades.

Suddenly, his thoughts were interrupted by Jack's hand pulling him sharply back.

"Don't put that

foot down," Jack warned. Kobe's left foot dangled in mid-air as he looked below it to where a huge gator lay partially hidden by undergrowth. Kobe was not normally scared of animals, but this was enormous! He gulped as the gator hissed at him.

7

Croc-o-dilicious

"I can't believe I didn't see him," said Kobe, amazed. "He's huge."

"How are we going to get past him?" Zia asked.

The giant gator was completely blocking the path, his tail in the murky pool to one side and his front legs stretched into the deep water on the other.

"It's okay," Jack reassured her. "You know

I'm good with animals."

"I wouldn't call these animals," she said, nervously.

"Well, they are," Jack told her. He slowly bent down toward the gator and began whispering to it, soothing it in sing-song tones. Its eyes went hazy, and it seemed to go into a trance. Edging closer, he put his hand on the creature's head and began stroking it. He pushed gently until the whole reptile disappeared into the deep water at the side of the path.

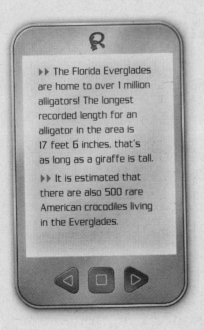

▶▶ The Florida Everglades are home to over 1 million alligators! The longest recorded length for an alligator in the area is 17 feet 6 inches, that's as long as a giraffe is tall.

▶▶ It is estimated that there are also 500 rare American crocodiles living in the Everglades.

"That was amazing," Zia told Jack, following him into a flat area of short grasses. Jack shrugged, as a huge fork of lightning

flashed in the graying sky.

"The storm's arrived," Zia observed. Suddenly, the sky darkened and rain began to fall in sheets around the agents.

"We should pitch one of the tents to keep dry," Jack suggested.

"We need to keep low to the ground," Zia told the others. "Make sure there are taller things nearby that will attract the lightning—close, but not too close!"

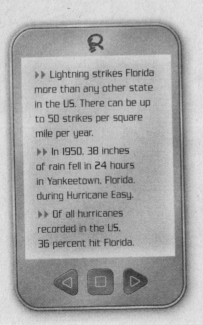

▶▶ Lightning strikes Florida more than any other state in the US. There can be up to 50 strikes per square mile per year.

▶▶ In 1950, 38 inches of rain fell in 24 hours in Yankeetown, Florida, during Hurricane Easy.

▶▶ Of all hurricanes recorded in the US, 36 percent hit Florida.

Kobe and Jack spotted a tall tree and helped Zia erect the tent nearby, all three working silently as the rain soaked them. When it was finished, they quickly dove inside, grateful for the shelter.

"How long do these storms last?" asked Kobe.

"It depends," Zia replied. "If we're just caught on the edge of it, it should pass in a few minutes. Otherwise it could last all afternoon."

"Great," Jack groaned.

It soon became obvious that the storm was not going to pass quickly; the rain just seemed to get heavier and faster. Zia counted the seconds between flashes of lightning and the crashes of thunder that followed.

"One Mississippi, two Mississippi, three Mississip—" she began as another crash echoed across the sky. "It's less than a mile away now."

"How can you tell?" asked Kobe.

"It takes about five seconds for the sound of thunder to travel a mile."

"So if you started counting to 20 Mississippis, and now you're at three ...?" Kobe's thought trailed off.

"It means that the storm's almost on top of us," Jack finished for him, as another flash lit up the whole tent. The thunder was immediate, followed by the loud crack of splintering wood. A flickering brightness shone into their tent, accompanied by intense heat.

Jack peered out to see the tree, cut down by lightning, now on fire. The rain was still falling

heavily, but the flames were somehow fighting the downpour and staying alight.

"Well, our tall tree has gone," Jack told the others.

"What are the poles in this tent made of?" Zia asked quickly.

"They felt like metal when I was carrying them," Kobe offered, shrugging.

If the tent poles were metal, they would attract the lightning now that the tall tree was gone. If the lightning were to hit the tent, everyone inside would be electrocuted. Zia made a decision; pushing past Kobe and Jack, she dashed outside. They called to her to come back but her mind was made up. Stopping nearby, Zia stood with her back to the tent and her arms held up above her head.

"What's she doing?" Jack asked. "Has she gone mad?"

"I don't know," replied Kobe. "Should one of us go after her?"

Before Jack could answer, an enormous fork of lightning erupted from the sky and struck Zia.

8

Rat Attack!

Jack and Kobe gasped as the lightning bolt hit Zia. Her hair shot up on end and the silver streak in it glowed bright white, like a fluorescent light. They both jumped up to help as she collapsed to the ground, but she started getting to her feet.

"I'm okay," she told them. "Stay in the tent."

"You don't look okay!" Kobe exclaimed.

"Don't come near me," Zia instructed sharply. "I'm still charged and could be dangerous."

The boys watched as Zia's hair slowly settled and the blazing white streak began to fade back to its usual silver-gray. When she was sure that the electricity had earthed, Zia ran back to the tent and crawled inside.

"We thought you were a goner," Jack told her.

"There was a moment when I thought so too," Zia admitted. "I've often wondered if my electromagnetic abilities let me absorb lightning. I've read about people who can in RIPLEY's files, but it's not something I'd ever tried myself."

▶▶ Park ranger Ray Sullivan was hit by lightning more times than anyone else. The strikes burned his toes, legs, stomach, chest, and set his hair on fire, but he survived them all before moving to a special home with lightning protection.

"You could have been fried!" Jack pointed out.

"All of us could have been fried," Zia explained. "Or as it turned out, you two could—I'd have been fine! There was no way I was going to be the one to break it to Mr. Cain that he had to find two new agents. Now it's getting dark and I'm starving! I wish we had something to eat."

"Oh, but we do," Jack told her, producing a rubbery-looking white bug that wiggled in his hand. "Beetle larvae. They're delicious!"

Zia and Kobe peered at the larva; it looked like a huge maggot. Zia wrinkled her nose, imagining how it would ooze as she bit into it.

"Just imagine it's a gummy worm," Kobe suggested, taking the bug and popping it into his mouth. "It's not as bad as you might think," he smiled.

After eating at Jack's 'Everglades Buffet,'

Zia was still not sure that beetle larvae would feature on her list of favorite foods, but she had to admit she was full and ready for a good night's sleep.

Kobe awoke the next morning to hear strange noises outside. A flurry of dark shapes scuttled around next to the canvas, and a small hole appeared at ground level, ragged as if it had been cut with tiny scissors. A furry, brown head with huge teeth poked through it, followed by a plump, downy body and a stringy tail. As more of the creatures rushed into his tent, Kobe quickly made his own way out.

"There are rats in my tent!" he yelled. Zia was standing outside her infested tent, too.

"We know," she told him. "But we have another problem."

Looking carefully around him, Kobe saw what Zia meant. He'd not noticed them to begin with, as their skins camouflaged them against the landscape, but hundreds of snakes were slithering toward them through the branches of trees, over logs, and across the ground.

"Where did they come from?" asked Kobe.

"They smelled the rats and have come out to find them," Jack explained. Kobe looked around; he could hear Jack, but he couldn't see him. Zia sighed and pointed upward; Jack was in a tree.

▶▶ Florida is now home to an African rat the size of a cat, after an exotic pet breeder let some loose. The giant rats weigh up to 10 pounds and it is feared that they could invade the whole state and cause major damage—even spreading unpleasant diseases such as monkeypox.

"He won't come down until the snakes are gone," she explained.

"You're really scared

of snakes?" Kobe asked, incredulously.

"I know, it's stupid," Jack admitted. "I can trek through the outback and eat all sorts of bugs, but there's just something about snakes. I had a bad experience with one when I was younger. I just couldn't seem to get it to understand me." He shivered at the thought. "From then on, I've always been a little scared of them."

"So the snakes are here for the rats, but how

did the rats get here?" Kobe asked, turning back to Zia.

"The rats were put here," she replied, pointing to a large wooden box. There were three more placed around the RBI camp. One of them still had a couple of rats inside, trying to climb up the steep sides.

"Surely, those boxes couldn't have held all these rats," said Kobe.

"Because of their collapsible skeletons, rats can fit into very tight spaces," came Jack's voice from the tree. "To force that many into such a small space is really cruel, but it could be done."

"But why would someone put rats around our camp?" Kobe asked. "Who even knows we're here?"

"DUL," Jack and Zia answered together.

"DUL knew that rats would attract snakes," Jack added.

"Are they all that big?" Zia asked suddenly, pointing to an enormous white snake with yellow markings that seemed to be moving over the other snakes.

▶▶ Burmese pythons can grow to over 20 feet and weigh over 400 pounds. In 1996 a 13-year-old boy from New York was suffocated by his 13-foot pet python when it mistook him for food.

▶▶ A nine-year-old python living in Florida measures 22 feet— and it's still growing!

"That's an albino Burmese python," said Jack. "Burmese pythons aren't native to Florida, but people keep them as pets. When they get too big, the owners set them free. Now there are loads because they have no natural enemies here—they've even been known to attack gators."

"Erm, Jack?" asked Zia warily. "Do they eat people?"

"There are reports of python owners being attacked," Jack told her. "But it's usually because the snakes have been mistreated, or they've mistaken their victim for food."

"So that snake coming right at us is nothing

to worry about?" Zia pointed at the large python that was pushing the smaller snakes out of the way and heading quickly toward the RBI agents, its menacing jaws wide open.

9

A Scaly Savior

"Jack, talk to it like you did the gator yesterday," Kobe suggested.

"I can't," Jack told him. "All snakes hear is my fear. After that first attempt, I've never managed to get a snake to understand me. But I'll give it a go."

Taking a deep breath, Jack moved toward a smaller snake slithering along a nearby branch. He began whispering to it, and for a moment, the snake was still.

"It's working," said Zia quietly. Then suddenly, the snake tried to strike, darting toward Jack's face so that he pulled away sharply and lost his balance. He teetered for a moment, grabbing wildly at branches, before tumbling into the marsh below.

"Are you okay?" Zia asked.

"Yeah, I'm fine," replied Jack, pulling leaves

from his hair. "But I hope someone has a plan B."

"I can't think of anything," said Zia, taking a step back from the approaching snake. As she did she heard a hiss, and turned to see three smaller snakes moving toward her from behind. "But we'd better come up with something quickly!"

The python moved closer and closer to the RBI agents, stalking its prey. It slithered around Kobe's ankle and his face paled.

"Just don't move," Jack instructed him. "It shouldn't attack if you keep perfectly still."

"I'm not moving," murmured Kobe, through tight lips. "And tell that to the python."

There was a sudden rustle in the trees, as if another creature was approaching, and a high-pitched squeal sounded all around them.

"What's that noise?" cried Zia, putting her hands over her ears.

The snakes froze and turned to face

something emerging from the tree line. Two large, green hands appeared, followed by what looked like a human head—but with a flat nose so that the face seemed reptilian. Raised ridges stuck out above its eyes, and its skin was covered in green scales. An equally scaly body followed, pulled low to the ground, with long back legs and a two-foot tail.

"It looks like a sort of Komodo dragon," whispered Kobe. "They've been known to eat people too."

The giant lizard's mouth was open; it was making the strange noise and inside its mouth Zia could make out a forked tongue. It moved toward Kobe, who now had the python wound round his leg. As the

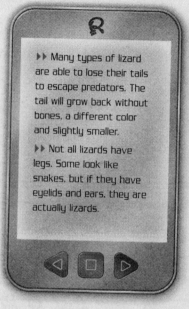

▶▶ Many types of lizard are able to lose their tails to escape predators. The tail will grow back without bones, a different color and slightly smaller.

▶▶ Not all lizards have legs. Some look like snakes, but if they have eyelids and ears, they are actually lizards.

creature approached, Kobe saw that its eyes also looked like a reptile's and he wasn't sure whether he should be more scared of it than the python. Slowly, it pushed itself up until it was standing on its hind legs.

Zia gasped. Kobe, on the other hand, felt his breathing stop completely. The six-foot creature was now standing over him, holding out what looked like a piece of old sheet. Closing his eyes, Kobe braced himself, expecting to feel the sheet go over his head, sure he was about to become the creature's evening meal ... but it didn't happen. He opened his eyes to see the creature gently cover the python's head instead, and then unwind the snake from his leg.

"Wait here," the creature told the agents, before disappearing again.

Believe it or not, the reptile had spoken! The RBI agents were so stunned by its normal, human-sounding voice that they were frozen to the spot.

"He's what we've been looking for, isn't he?" Zia whispered.

"I think so," Jack replied. "Isn't he amazing?"

"Surely we should be following him?" Kobe suggested. Jack and Zia nodded.

"How will we know where he's gone?" Zia asked, looking to Kobe, their expert tracker. Kobe pulled their heat sensor from his pocket.

"I don't think I need any special talents for this one," he told them.

"Good thinking," Jack agreed. "The talking lizard should have a different heat signature to the snakes. I'm sure he's warm-blooded, like us."

"Something like that?" Kobe asked, pointing to a reddish blob moving across the screen.

"Exactly like that," said Jack. "Let's go."

The three agents set off in pursuit, all the time watching the marbled heat-blob on the sensor screen. They crossed streams and grassy lowlands until they reached mangrove trees, where the blob stopped. The lizard man had reached his destination.

Kobe looked around. Amid the dense trees was what looked like a wooden shack, but it was almost completely covered in vines, making it very difficult to see. As they approached it and looked for a door, a voice sounded from the trees.

"I told you to stay where you were," it said. "What are you doing here?"

The agents looked for the source of the voice. The lizard man dropped down from a tree; he had been very well camouflaged.

"We came to find you," Jack replied. The

man-lizard looked at him quizzically.

As quickly as he could, Jack explained about the RBI; how they were here to seek out wondrous things, and that they had been searching for days to discover the truth behind the reported sightings.

"You'd better come in then," the lizard told them, opening a concealed vine-covered door.

The inside of the shack was extraordinary: it looked like one of the rooms at Ripley High. Every wall was covered with unusual things. A huge alligator skin was stretched across one of the walls. It must have been nearly 25 feet long! Next to it was an enormous alligator jawbone, an ancient-looking boomerang, a table covered with the remains of a Burmese python skin, and a large collection of tennis balls.

"Wow," said Kobe in awe. "This is incredible."

"Kobe likes artifacts," Zia explained.

"May I look around?" Kobe asked.

"Feel free," said the lizard man.

"What are the tennis balls for?" asked Jack. "I can't imagine there are many tennis courts in the Everglades."

"Alligators will eat anything," the lizard man

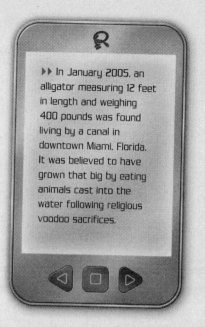

▶▶ In January 2005, an alligator measuring 12 feet in length and weighing 400 pounds was found living by a canal in downtown Miami, Florida. It was believed to have grown that big by eating animals cast into the water following religious voodoo sacrifices.

explained. "I found one who had sucked up so many tennis balls that he was constantly afloat and couldn't dive! I operated on the poor thing and kept the balls as a souvenir—and to make sure the gator didn't swallow them all again!"

"Wow," said Jack. "That must have been one hungry gator."

"So, what do you want to know?" asked the lizard man.

"We want to know all about you. Who you

are, how you came to look so unique, and how the Everglades became your home," Zia replied.

"My name is Joshua Tucker," he began, going on to describe how he had never really gotten along with humans. He just didn't understand people, and there weren't many who understood him. Having trained as a vet, he had always loved reptiles, and had dedicated his life to the study and preservation of this

often misunderstood, but gentle, species.

About ten years ago, he had researched the Seminole Indians and discovered that they had lived alongside nature in the Everglades for centuries. He decided that living among reptiles would allow him to study and protect them in their natural environment. (The Burmese python they came across earlier, for example, was never meant to live in the Everglades, so Joshua did everything he could

to make its transition easier.) When he altered his appearance to fit in more, he found that he felt happier with each change. He tattooed his body with green scales, grew his nails long to look like claws, modified his tongue, had his nose smoothed down, finally, he had the tail added. Joshua wiggled it to emphasize the point.

"It took a little while to get used to," he told them, "but now I couldn't live without it." The Everglades provided everything he needed and he rarely had to venture out. "Although I do sometimes miss real food," he added, bowing his head. "I'm sorry—it was me who stole your rations."

"I knew I saw something that night!" said Zia.

Jack asked Joshua all the things they would need to know for the database and their debriefing: his age, weight, and height, and unusual characteristics (other than the obvious ones!), while Kobe was eagerly scanning the shelves of astonishing artifacts. His attention was drawn to one particular object at the back: a small, gnarled statue. It was about 18 inches long and covered in dust.

"This is the missing mermaid from Artifact Studies," he told Zia.

As he picked up the dried creature, pictures flashed into his mind; echoes of the artifact's long history and images of the people who had come into contact with it. Part of Kobe's unique ability was to understand the history of a person or object just by touch, and this relic was no different.

"I can feel Ripley's presence here," he told the others. "He held on to this for a long time. It's definitely the missing artifact."

The agents said goodbye to Joshua and promised to keep in touch, before heading back to Ripley High for a debriefing with Mr. Cain and RIPLEY.

10

Believe It or Not!

"I can't believe that Joshua let me keep the mermaid," said Kobe.

"He was really nice," added Zia. "People thought he was a monster. It's terrible."

"You thought he was a monster," Jack teased her, "when you first saw him."

"I didn't see him," Zia argued. "If I had, I would have given him the food anyway."

"Don't forget that he said he was happy to be

part of the RIPLEY's database too," said Jack.

"As long as we promised to bring him real food whenever we were in Florida," Zia laughed.

"Wow," said Max, seeing Kobe's new find. "Is that one of the lost artifacts?"

"It's not lost anymore," he smiled. "I know the best place for it. In fact, I'm going to go and display it right now."

Kate went with Kobe to the school's 'Odditorium'. It was full of the treasures that Robert Ripley had discovered on his travels.

"There's always been an empty pedestal in here," Kobe explained, as he dusted off a Greek column-style stand with sunken circles on the top. "I thought it was mysterious that this was the only one with nothing on it."

"It looks like the new, um, thing, would fit exactly into one of those circles," commented Kate. Kobe placed the creature so that its shape fit the indentation.

"Wow," said Kate, seeing how perfectly it

matched. There was a whirr from the pedestal and a small drawer popped out from underneath the artifact. Kate reached in to find a letter and an intricately designed red and yellow tin.

"It's a letter from Robert Ripley," she told Kobe, before reading it out:

To those who follow me,

If you have found this letter than you are already living up to my expectations and the quest has begun!

As I'm sure you will know, I was something of an explorer and I loved to collect unusual things on my travels. You will hopefully find most of them around the school.

However, a few of those objects were too unique to be left to fall into the wrong hands. There are those who wish to stop my work and to keep others from appreciating the wonder of the truly fantastic (particularly an organization calling itself 'DUL'). If you are true believers in the unbelievable, then it is time for my treasures to once more be found and returned.

The first of my concealed artifacts will have led you to this message, and with this letter you will find your first clue. It, along with four more, will give you the location of the next hidden artifact. I expect you to prove yourselves worthy followers, with the same spirit of adventure that I possessed!

Believe it or not, you will know the clues when you come across them — but be prepared to look in unexpected places along the way.

The hunt is on!

Robert Ripley

Kobe and Kate took the letter and tin back to the RBI base.

"There is no information in my system about these hidden artifacts," RIPLEY told them. "But the handwriting does match samples of Rip's writing that we have on file."

Excitedly, Kobe opened the tin. Inside was a photograph of Robert Ripley in the snow. Although the photograph was in black and white, it was possible to make out the Aurora Borealis, the Northern Lights, in the sky above him.

"How is this photograph a clue?" Kate asked indignantly. "It's just Rip in the snow."

"Is that a penguin?" asked Zia pointing to a tiny black speck in the photo.

"Don't be silly," said Jack. "Penguins live in the South Pole and this is the North Pole. You can see the Northern Lights."

"Oh, I thought it might have helped us," said Zia.

"Rip said that there would be other clues," Max reminded them. "Maybe once we have more, this one will make sense."

"We don't even know where to look for the other four clues," Li complained.

"Our main mission is to add to the RIPLEY's database," Mr. Cain explained, "and to protect the information already in it. We carry on with our missions as usual—it may be that you will find other clues on these missions, as you will be following in the footsteps of your mentor to far-flung corners of the world. But we must put the database first. It's why the RBI exists, after all."

"But we can keep our eyes open at the same time," said Jack, cheerily.

"Of course," Mr. Cain agreed. "Now, Kate, Li, Alek—we have a new mission for you. RIPLEY has some new information on ...."

As Mr. Cain briefed the other agents, Max and Kobe were both still thinking about the artifact hunt. Kobe was excited about all the new artifacts they might discover—what could make them so special that Rip would hide them? Max was just thrilled by the prospect of a treasure hunt and an adventure. Of course, all their missions were adventures, but this added an extra element of mystery. He thought about what Rip had told them.

"The hunt is on ..." he smiled.

RIPLEY'S DATABASE ENTRY

RIPLEY FILE NUMBER: 22651

MISSION BRIEF : Believe it or not, sightings of a strange reptilian creature have been reported by witnesses in the Florida Everglades. Investigate accuracy of these accounts and collect factual information for Ripley database.

CODE NAME : Lizard Man

REAL NAME : Joshua Tucker

LOCATION : Florida, USA

AGE : 34

HEIGHT : 6 ft 1 inch

WEIGHT : 182 lb

VIDEO CAPTURE

UNUSUAL CHARACTERISTICS:

Body covered in carved scales, painted green; forked tongue; nose smoothed down; working tail added to lower back; eyes tattooed yellow with permanent reptilian lenses; implants under skin like horns

RBI DATABASE APPROVED!

INVESTIGATING AGENTS :

Jack Stevens, Zia Mendoza, Kobe Shakur

▶▶ YOUR NEXT ASSIGNMENT

JOIN THE RBI IN THEIR NEXT ADVENTURE!

THE DRAGON'S TRIANGLE

Prologue

"Isn't it beautiful, Riki?" Aimi asked, as she watched the sun sink lower over the North Pacific Ocean.

"It would be better if that mist cleared," said Riki. He had been so pleased with his idea to take Aimi to see the sunset, hoping she would find it really romantic. Now the two of them were sitting in his car, and a sea mist had appeared out of nowhere, hiding the setting sun behind it.

"But don't you think it's amazing, the way the sun is so bright that it's burning through all that horrible mist?" asked Aimi. "It's like a glowing ruby, smoldering its way through an enchanted smog."

Riki frowned at his girlfriend's description and looked carefully to see what she meant; he did see a glowing ruby, two of them in fact. Twin spheres of red light were blazing through the mist, and they seemed to be moving.

"I don't think that's the sun," he said, peering ahead to make out the source of the lights. They were too close together for car headlights but they were definitely moving toward them. "Maybe we should come back tomorrow?"

Riki could see the disappointment on Aimi's face as she stared out into the haze; but then her expression changed to one of fear. He looked out the window as she let out a piercing scream. A dark shape was emerging from the fog. Riki couldn't make out what it was, but the glowing red lights were definitely eyes. In a panic, he turned the ignition key, but the engine wouldn't start.

"What's wrong?" asked Aimi.

Riki silently cursed his old car. The sea mist was affecting the ancient engine.

"Riki, I want to go," Aimi pleaded.

"I think we need to run," he told her, throwing open the car door. Aimi did the same, and Riki ran around the car and grabbed her hand. He pulled her with him as he ran away from the car and the strange creature closing in on it.

Only seconds later, Riki felt a blast of hot air scorch his back and neck. Aimi tripped and fell, and as he bent down to help her up, he turned back to see the source of the heat. The huge dark shape was now right where they had been. Flames were streaming from its mouth and Riki's car had been consumed in a giant ball of flames.

►► ENTER THE STRANGE WORLD OF RIPLEY'S ...

►► Believe it or not, there is a lot of truth in this remarkable tale. The Ripley's team travels the globe to track down true stories that will amaze you. Read on to find out about real Ripley's case files and discover incredible facts about some of the extraordinary people and places in our world.

Ripley's Believe It or Not!®

▶▶ LEOPARD MAN

Known as the Leopard Man of Skye, Tom Leppard from Scotland has had his entire body tattooed with the markings of a big cat.

▶▶ For over 15 years Leopard Man lived in a hut made from sticks and stones, on the island of Skye.

▶▶ Before he moved into a regular house in 2008, Leopard Man used to bathe in the river.

▶▶ He has had more than 99 percent of his body tattooed—only the skin between his toes and the insides of his ears remain untouched!

credit: Ian Waldie/Rex Features

▶▶ Every week tattooed Tom Leppard would travel three miles by canoe to a nearby town for his supplies.

credit: © John Anderson—Fotolia.com

THE EVERGLADES

▶▶ The Florida Everglades is a vast area of shallow wetlands that is home to dangerous alligators and escaped Burmese pythons.

▶▶ In 2000, a man got lost in the Everglades and spent the night taped to a tree branch to escape alligators.

▶▶ While riding a jet ski on the Suwannee River in Florida in 2006, a man was knocked unconscious when a 4-foot sturgeon jumped out of the water and hit him.

▶▶ In 1979, a 10,000-year-old boomerang-type weapon was discovered in the 'glades, and scientists believe that well-preserved bodies from thousands of years ago could also be hidden in the murky depths.

▶▶ In 2007, a photographer spent 53 hours lost in the Everglades without food or water after being scared by an alligator. She was eventually found just a mile from her car.

▶▶ Lake Okeechobee in the 'glades is 20 times the size of the city of Miami.

>> By changing himself into an animal, Catman says he's following an old Native American tradition.

>> CATMAN

Stalking Cat, also known as Dennis Avner, from Nevada, is transforming himself into a tiger through extensive plastic surgery.

>> Catman, as he is commonly known, developed his obsession with all things feline at the age of 23.

>> He is covered in striped tattoos to look like a tiger.

>> Cat's surgeries have changed his upper lip, and given him pointed ears, whiskers and real fangs.

▶▶ Alligators and crocodiles are the only reptiles that roar, and these terrifying sounds can be heard over long distances.

▶▶ U.S. president John Quincy Adams kept a pet alligator in the East Room of the White House for months.

ALLIGATOR

credit: © Earl Robbins—Fotolia.com

▶▶ An alligator can be hypnotized in 30 seconds by applying pressure to its eyeballs with the fingertips!

▶▶ Clarence Birdseye, the inventor of processed frozen food, once tried to freeze a whole alligator!

▶▶ In 2005, an unfortunate six-foot alligator was swallowed whole by a 13-foot Burmese python in the Florida Everglades. The snake burst, however, when the eaten gator clawed a hole in its stomach. Neither animal survived the experience.

CASE FILE #003

▶▶ LIZARDMAN

Erik Sprague, an entertainer from New York State, has spent many years changing his body to look like a lizard!

▶▶ Erik has always loved lizards and always wanted to look like one.

▶▶ His body changes began with ear-piercing at the age of 18.

▶▶ Now he has stretched ear-lobes, a forked tongue, sharp teeth, and scaly green tattoos all over!

▶▶ The Lizardman has permanent silicone implants on his head, just like real gnarled lizard skin.

▶▶ RIPLEY

▶▶ In his lifetime, Ripley traveled over 450,000 miles looking for oddities—the distance from Earth to the Moon and back again.

▶▶ Ripley had a large collection of cars, but he couldn't drive. He also bought a Chinese sailing boat, called Mon Lei, but he couldn't swim.

▶▶ Ripley was so popular that his weekly mailbag often exceeded 170,000 letters, all full of weird and wacky suggestions for his cartoon strip.

▶▶ He kept a 28-foot-long boa constrictor as a pet in his New York home.

▶▶ Ripley's Believe It or Not! cartoon is the longest-running cartoon strip in the world, read in 42 countries and 17 languages every day.

In 1918, Robert Ripley became fascinated by strange facts while he was working as a cartoonist at the *New York Globe*. He was passionate about travel and, by 1940, had visited no less than 201 countries, gathering artifacts and searching for stories that would be right for his column, which he named Believe It or Not!

Ripley bought an island estate at Mamaroneck, New York, and filled the huge house there with unusual objects and odd creatures that he'd collected on his explorations.

RIPLEY'S **RBI** FACT OR FICTION? BUREAU of INVESTIGATION

PACKED WITH FUN & GAMES, THE **RBI** WEBSITE IS HERE! CHECK IT OUT

FUN!

REVIEWS

DOWNLOADS

MAPS & DATA

MORE TEAM TALK

THE NEXT FILES